Our
Gracie
Aunt

Text copyright © 2002 by Jacqueline Woodson
Illustrations copyright © 2002 by Jon J Muth

First Edition
1 3 5 7 9 10 8 6 4 2

Printed in Singapore

Library of Congress Cataloging-in-Publication Data
Woodson, Jacqueline.
Our Gracie Aunt / by Jacqueline Woodson; illustrations by Jon J Muth.
p.   cm.
Summary: When a brother and sister are taken to stay with their mother's sister
because their mother neglects them, they wonder if they will see their mother again.
ISBN 0-7868-0620-6 (trade)
[1. Brothers and sisters—Fiction. 2. Child abuse—Fiction. 3. Aunts—Fiction.
4. Afro-Americans—Fiction.] I. Muth, Jon J, ill. II. Title.
PZ7. W868 Ou 2002   [Fic]—dc21   00-39721

Visit www.jumpatthesun.com

Our Gracie Aunt

BY JACQUELINE WOODSON
ILLUSTRATIONS BY JON J MUTH

JUMP AT THE SUN

HYPERION BOOKS FOR CHILDREN

NEW YORK

When the lady
came that night,
Debee was in the
kitchen making
sandwiches.
The lady said,
"My name is Miss
Ivy. I want to talk
to your mama."
"Don't open
that door, Johnson,"
Debee said.
So I didn't.

When Miss Roy came the next morning, we
were both asleep on the couch.
"You have to open the door," she said.
"Not for strangers, we don't," Beebee said back.

I looked under the doo
I could see Miss Roy's shoe
They were nic

"Where's your mama?" Miss Roy
wanted to know.

Beebee got real quiet. After a while she
said, "She went someplace."

"How long has she been gone?"

I counted the days on my fingers.

"Since a few minutes ago," Beebee said.

"Well, I'll be back this afternoon," Miss
Roy said. "And if your mama's not home,
I'll have to take you with me. It's not safe
to leave little kids alone."

"I'm not a little kid," Beebee said.

But Miss Roy's nice shoes were already
click-clacking down the hall.

"You think Mama's ever coming home, Bee?"

Beebee frowned. "She always did before, right?"

Sometimes my mama went away for a day. Sometimes for a lot of days. That's how it was with our mama.

"You know where Miss Roy wants to take us?" Beebee said. "Foster care. It's when you live with somebody that's not your mama."

"They have toys in foster care, Beebee?"

Beebee looked kind of sad. "Sometimes."

When Miss Roy came in the afternoon, Beebee finally opened the door.

Miss Roy was tall like Mama.

"You must be Bernadette," she said to Beebee.

"Everybody calls me Beebee, though."

"Beebee," Miss Roy said. "I like that. And you must be Johnson."

I was hiding behind the couch, but I stuck my head out and nodded.

"I don't have another name," I said.

Miss Roy smiled.

She had a pretty smile, Miss Roy did.

"How come you already know our names?" Beebee asked. She gave Miss Roy one of her looks. Beebee had all kinds of looks she could give people.

"A neighbor called and said that you'd been alone a while," Miss Roy said. "My job is to make sure little kids get taken care of."

"I'm not a little kid," Beebee said.

I didn't say anything. It seemed like a nice job, the one Miss Roy had.

Miss Roy helped Beebee put some stuff in a bag for us. Even though I told her not to, she brought Bluey.

"I'm too big for that," I said.

"Let's take it anyway." Beebee was trying to sound like a grown-up. Showing off for Miss Roy.

"What about when Mama comes and we're not here?" I asked. "What if she can't find us?"

"I'll leave her a note." Miss Roy had one already written up. She put it on the table under the saltshaker.

When we walked outside, Miss Clyde from across the street said, "You all be good, you hear?"

Miss Clyde always kept an eye on us. Sometimes, she brought food over.

"I'm hungry," I whispered to Beebee. She gave me one of her mean looks.

Miss Roy had a shiny white car. She made both of us sit in the back with the seat belts on.

"I was able to get in touch with your aunt Gracie," Miss Roy said. Beebee just shrugged and stared out the window, but I looked right at Miss Roy and asked her who this Gracie aunt was.

"Mama's sister." Beebee's voice was real quiet. "How do you know about her?" she asked Miss Roy.

"I talked to some neighbors," Miss Roy said. "I did some searching and found her on the other side of town."

"Mama doesn't like Aunt Gracie," Beebee said.

I folded my arms and frowned. "How do you know her?"

"You know her too, Johnson. You probably just don't remember, 'cause you were real small the last time we saw her."

"Your aunt Gracie's a good person," Miss Roy said. "I know she'll take care of you."

"My *mama* can take care of us!" Beebee said. She stuck out her bottom lip. We all got real quiet.

After a while, Miss Roy stopped at a restaurant.

"Can I have anything I want?" I asked.

Miss Roy nodded and touched my head. Her hand felt nice there.

"Our mama knows where our Gracie aunt lives?" I asked.

Miss Roy nodded again.

"So she'll be able to come get us when she gets home, right?"

Miss Roy said, "We'll see."

Miss Roy drove us to a big house near the river. A
woman came out, drying her hands on her jeans. She
stood on the porch looking at us and shaking her head like
she couldn't believe it.

I couldn't believe it either. There was a tire on a rope
hanging from a tree. And one of those red cars you get in
and pedal. And pretty flowers everywhere.

"You don't even miss Mama," Beebee said. She was mad
because I was looking at all of our Gracie aunt's stuff.

"Do too." And I did, way deep down inside.

Our Gracie aunt hugged me and Beebee. I hugged her
back because I liked the way she smelled—like something
sweet cooking on the stove. But Beebee stayed stiff.

"I have some cookies baking—with your names on
them," our Gracie aunt said.

Then Beebee smiled. It was a little tiny smile.
But I saw it.

That night, our Gracie aunt said, "I want to tuck you all in."

"What's *tuck in*?"

Our Gracie aunt pulled the cover tight around me and made sure my head felt good on the pillow.

"That's *tuck in*," she whispered, kissing my forehead.

I liked tuck in. "Beebee needs tuck in, too."

"No, I don't," Beebee said. Then she turned her head toward the wall and didn't say anything else.

Our Gracie aunt sat on the edge of my bed and sang a song about birds watching over us. It was a pretty song. Beebee turned her head a little. She was listening, too.

The next morning Beebee asked, "How come you never came to see us if you're our aunt?"

"You know how you and Johnson argue sometimes? Well, me and your mama did, too," our Gracie aunt said. "We stopped speaking to each other a long time ago. I don't even remember what we were arguing about. Then me and your mama lost touch."

"But how come you didn't get back *in* touch?" Beebee asked.

After a long time, our Gracie aunt said, "You all moved a couple of times, and I didn't know where you were anymore. I even tried to call you."

"We don't have a phone," I said.

"I know," our Gracie aunt said.

Beebee rolled her eyes up to the ceiling. "People all the time making excuses about going away."

"Just because a person goes away," our Gracie aunt said, "doesn't mean they don't love you."

"What does it mean, then?" Beebee asked.

It just means they'll be back! I wanted to yell.

"I wish I knew," our Gracie aunt said.

"What did you love about Mama?" Beebee whispered.

"She was a good big sister. When we were little, I loved everything about her."

And Beebee said, "Me, too."

"Yeah," I said. "Me, too."

Sometimes our Gracie
aunt let us help her cook.
She let us throw
spaghetti against the wall.
it stuck, it was done.

And Saturday nights, she made popcorn and let us watch scary movies with her.

When the vegetables were ready, we picked them from the garden.

And when I cried about missing Mama, our Gracie aunt gave me Bluey to hold.

"It's good to cry," she'd say. "Crying washes you out inside."

Some days me and Beebee sat crying, washing ourselves out inside.

One day, me and Beebee were out playing when Miss Roy drove up. She went into the house and talked to our Gracie aunt for a few minutes.

"Johnson and Beebee," Miss Roy said. "I need you to come with me for a while. Your mother wants to see you."

Me and Beebee ran to her car.

The whole way, we were jumping up and down in our seats.

"We're going to see Mama!" Beebee whispered.

I smiled. Mama had come back to us just like I knew she would.

Miss Roy drove us
to a tall building.
  "You go right in there
to the first room," she
said when we got inside.
"I'll wait here for you."

Mama looked different. She looked smaller and sad.
I held tighter to Beebee's hand.

"Hi, Mama." Beebee leaned over and kissed Mama.
Then she squeezed my hand, and I whispered "Hi" and
kissed her, too.

I thought about the tire swing in our Gracie aunt's
yard. I thought about me and Beebee not even saying
good-bye to our Gracie aunt. Then I thought about all
the nights me and Beebee didn't eat 'cause we didn't
have any food and we didn't know where Mama was. I
wanted to go back to our Gracie aunt. There was always
something to eat at her house. Every night she gave me
a tuck-in. And even though we're big, some nights our
Gracie aunt let me and Beebee sit on her lap. Just the
three of us sitting quiet and hugging. Our Gracie aunt
said, *Everybody needs a little love sometimes.*

"Even when a mama loves you, she can't always take care of you. Sometimes she has to go away," Mama said.

"I know," Beebee said.

"I know," I said.

Even though I really didn't.

"We going home?"

Mama shook her head. "Not right now, Johnson. But when we go home it'll be for always. Your aunt Gracie's going to take good care of you until I can again."

"When's that going to be?"

"Soon," Mama promised.

I took my red truck out of my pocket and gave it to Mama.

"You can keep it, if you want to."

Mama held it against her cheek and smiled.

"You all just remember that I love you, okay? Will you remember that?"

Me and Beebee nodded.

"Our Gracie aunt told us," I said. "That you loved us, and stuff."

"Gracie's a good person," Mama said.

Beebee wiped her eyes. "You're good too, Mama."

Late, late in the afternoon, me and Beebee climbed out of Miss Roy's car. Our Gracie aunt was standing on the porch smiling. We ran as fast as we could up those stairs.

"Do you love us?" I asked.

And our Gracie aunt nodded.

"Do you have to go away?" Beebee wanted to know.

She pulled us to her and held us tight. "I don't have to go anywhere but here for now!"

"You're our Gracie aunt for always, right?"

"Yes I am, Johnson. I'm your aunt Gracie for always."

"Aunt Gracie," I whispered. Then I said it a little louder. "Aunt Gracie."

And we hugged for a long, long time.